HORRIBLE HARRY
GOES TO
THE MOON

HORRIBLE HARRY
GOES TO
THE MOON

BY SUZY KLINE
Pictures by Frank Remkiewicz

SCHOLASTIC INC.
New York Toronto London Auckland Sydney
Mexico City New Delhi Hong Kong Buenos Aires

Dedicated to my first grandchild,
Jacob Matthew DeAngelis,
born July 2, 1999,
Manchester, New Hampshire.
Jacob,
I love you.
Grandma Sue

ISBN 0-439-19396-6

12 11 10 9 8 7 6 5 4 3 2 1   1 2 3 4 5 6/0

Printed in the U.S.A.   40

First Scholastic printing, September 2001

Set in New Century Schoolbook

Acknowledgments:
Special appreciation to . . .
my editor, Cathy Hennessy, for her valuable help
with this story.
my third grade class of 1998–99 who first took
me to the moon, and my aide, Colleen Combs,
who came along with us.
Julie Pagano, speech therapist, whose "tag sale"
telescope opened up a whole new world on that
full moon November night.
David Morse, spokesman for NASA, for his kind
help.

Contents

Who Gets to Sit on the Moon?

I'll never forget the month of October in third grade. That was when Harry took me to the moon.

I know it sounds crazy, but he *did*.

Harry took me to the moon.

This is how it all started . . .

It was a Monday. We were sitting on the rug having our morning conversation when Miss Mackle said, "I have a surprise for you, class."

We all looked at the teacher.

She had a *huge* brown package. It was bigger than my desk. "What's that?" Sidney blurted out.

"An inspiration," Miss Mackle said. "And it was on sale at Big Mart."

Slowly, the teacher unwrapped the brown packaging. It was a purple couch made of three cushions. When we saw the bright yellow moons on it, we went "Ooooooooh!"

We watched the teacher open up the couch and lay it flat on the floor. Then she sat on it. Now the couch looked like an air mattress with a comfy place for your head.

Harry sat down next to her. "Neat-o!" he said. "I'm sitting on the moon!"

"You mean the purple couch with yellow moons on it," Mary explained as she plopped down on the other side of the teacher.

"Hey, I get to sit here too," Sidney protested.

Then he sat on Mary.

"Ouch!" Mary groaned. "Get off, Sid! I was here first."

"Okay, boys and girls," Miss Mackle replied. "How can we make this fair?"

Harry flashed a toothy smile. "It seems fair to me right now."

Everyone frowned except Song Lee. She giggled. Mary pushed Sidney off.

"I have an idea," I said.

"Yes, Doug?" Miss Mackle replied.

"We have a monitor chart. We could make sitting on the couch a job."

"Cool," Dexter said.

Miss Mackle laughed. "A job? Well, I guess it could be for one day."

"And if we go in ABC order," Mary suggested, "it would be *really* fair."

Miss Mackle nodded.

"I figured it out," I said. "If there are twenty-one kids in the class, and only two get to sit on the couch each day, everyone gets a turn once every two weeks."

"Good math, Doug!" Miss Mackle said. "But is there a remainder?"

We all thought about it.

Mary replied first. "There's a remainder of one." Then she paused. "I wonder . . . *who* the *last person* in ABC order would be in our class? The person who has to wait *three weeks* for a turn."

Everyone looked around while Mary continued thinking aloud. "That would be Shoshanna White, but she moved last month. So . . . that means . . . *Spooger* would be the remainder."

Everyone stared at Harry.

"HARRY SPOOGER'S LAST!" Sidney shouted.

"No I'm not, Sid the Squid. You are!" Harry replied.

"Hey, nicknames don't count," Sidney snapped.

Mary ignored the boys and looked at Ida. "We get to go first," she sang.

Their last names were Berg and Burrell.

Harry folded his arms. "I'm not leaving. I was here first. We can start the ABC order *tomorrow.*"

"*Excuuuuuuse* me," Ida said as she stood over him.

Harry didn't budge.

"Harry?" Miss Mackle said. "Your turn will be coming up."

"Yeah, once in a blue moon," he grumbled.

"Interesting," Miss Mackle said. "Do you know what that means, Harry? Once in a blue moon?"

"Yeah. Doesn't everybody?"

Mary leaned forward. She wanted to know, but she wasn't going to ask. Harry licked his lips. He loved secrets. "I know lots of stuff about the moon. I watch the science guy on TV every day after school."

"Hmmm," Miss Mackle said. "How many of you would like to collect some facts about the moon?"

Everyone waved their hands in the air.

"I know where to find some," Mary said, getting up. "In our green science book." Then she went over to her desk.

Harry jumped up and pointed to his brain. "I bet I have more moon facts in my noodle than you do in that old book."

Mary laughed. "You don't know anything about the moon!"

"Do too!" Harry said.

"Do not!" Mary replied.

Miss Mackle smiled. I bet she was glad they weren't fighting over the couch anymore. Now they were just fighting over the moon.

Ten minutes later, Ida and Dexter brought eight moon books from the library. Song Lee and I went over to the computer and got on the Internet.

Harry went to the closet and got out the big box of old newspapers and magazines. After he rummaged around for a while, he pulled out two sections of a newspaper. The classifieds and the comics. "Cool!" he said.

"You'll never find moon facts *there*," Mary scolded.

"I just did," Harry said, cutting something out.

Mary took off her glasses. "Harry Spooger, I wish you would go to the moon!"

"What, Mary?"

"I said . . . I wish *you* would go to the moon!"

"Hmmmm . . ." Harry mumbled. "I'll think about that."

While Harry nodded his head, Mary rolled her eyes.

Jokes and Jumps!

All that week everyone collected moon facts.

Except Sidney.

He kept going around the room cracking dumb jokes. "When is a door not a door?"

A few of us looked up.

"When it's a jar! Get it?" Sidney cackled.

Mary didn't laugh. "Sidney La Fleur, we are busy studying the moon. Your joke has nothing to do with space. So get lost!"

Sidney scowled as he wandered over to the old newspaper and magazine box. He pulled out a *Reader's Digest* and flipped through it. "Hey," he said. "They have jokes in here. Cool."

At least Sidney stopped pestering us.

During math time, we took turns lining up by the chalkboard. We got a

piece of chalk and marked how high we could reach.

"Don't stand on your toes," Miss Mackle said. "Just make a chalk mark as high as you can."

We did that.

"Remember to record the next mark as you jump. Ready? Set? *Jump!*" Miss Mackle called.

Three of us jumped into the air as

high as we could. We made a quick mark on the board when we were at the top of our leap.

"I bet I jumped the highest!" Harry bragged.

Miss Mackle used a ruler to measure the space between the two chalk marks. She rounded it off to make it easy.

"Whoa!" Harry exclaimed. "I jumped one foot!"

"That means you'd jump *six feet* on the moon," Mary said. "Because there's six times less gravity. It said that in our green science book."

"I jumped ten inches!" Song Lee said.

"That's sixty inches on the moon or *five feet,*" I added. "Same as me!"

When Mary finally jumped, she barely got off the ground. "Four inches," Miss Mackle said softly.

"Four times six is twenty-four inches," I whispered. I didn't want to embarrass Mary. Everyone else had jumped higher than her.

"TWO FEET on the moon," Harry shouted.

"Thanks, Harry *Spooger!*" Mary groaned.

"Hey Mary," Sidney interrupted. "I know what you need—a good joke. This one's about outer space."

Mary took off her glasses. "N . . . O . . . spells NO!" she shouted.

Miss Mackle took a step back.

Song Lee tried to cheer Mary up. "I drew this for you." Then she handed Mary a picture of them jumping rope on a sunny day.

Mary managed to smile a little.

After everyone had a turn to jump, Miss Mackle looked around the room.

Sidney had his head down. He looked pretty sad.

"I think we need a break," Miss Mackle said as she walked over to Sidney's desk. "Does anyone know a joke about outer space?"

Sidney's head popped up like a red fishing bobber.

"I do! I found one in *Reader's Digest*.

It's about heaven. That's *out there* in space like the moon."

"Puleeeze," Mary moaned.

"It must be a good one then, Sidney. Tell it to us," Miss Mackle said with a smile.

"I have it memorized," Sidney bragged. Then he walked up to the front of the room.

"Well, Sam and Mike were friends. They both loved sports. They grew up together. Even when they were old, they hung out together. Then one day when Sam was ninety, he died."

The class was pin quiet.

Sidney continued, *"A year later, Sam looked down from heaven at his friend Mike.*

"'Hey, Mike. It's me.'

"'Is that you, Sam?'

"'Yup, I'm up here in heaven.'

"'What's it like up there?'

"'Well there's good news and bad news.'

"'What's the good news?'

"'We play baseball everyday in heaven.'

"'Great! What's the bad news?'

"'You're pitching tomorrow.'"

When Sidney finished, Harry slapped his knee. "That *was* a good one, Sid!"

Song Lee and Miss Mackle giggled.

"I don't get it," Mary said.

"Well," Harry explained. "If Mike's pitching tomorrow, it means he's going to die next and join Sam in heaven."

"Oh," Mary replied.

"You have to use your noodle," Harry said, pointing to his brain.

"Oh, Harry!" Mary snapped. "Why don't you go to the moon!"

"Hey, I've been thinking about that. I just need to work on a few details, like . . . how to get there, and when's the best time for takeoff."

Mary looked at Harry in disbelief. Then she broke out laughing.

"Now *that's* the best joke I've heard today!" she said.

The Suitcase

The following Monday, Miss Mackle pulled something out from under her desk.

A brown suitcase.

"Where are you going?" Sidney blurted out.

"To the moon," she replied.

Everyone raised their eyebrows.

Harry leaned forward on his desk.

"What did you pack?" Sidney asked.

"I'll show you," she said, and she held up each item. "Suntan lotion, dark glasses, insect repellent, a swimsuit, an umbrella, golf clubs, and a paper fan." Then she fanned herself.

"So, what do you think?" Miss Mackle asked. "Did I do a good job packing for the moon?"

"You don't need insect repellent!" Mary scoffed. "It says in our green science book that there's no life on the moon, so there's no bees or mosquitoes or bugs up there." She walked up and pointed.

Miss Mackle took out the insect repellent. "Okay, I'll leave that here."

Dexter raised his hand to speak next. "You don't need those dark glasses. I found out how hot it gets on the moon. Something like two hundred and fifty degrees Fahrenheit. Man, that's too hot for sunbathing. You can forget the suntan lotion too."

"Yeah," Harry agreed. "You wear that swimsuit on the moon and you'll crisp up like a potato chip."

"Do you have to be so gross?" Mary replied.

"Good research!" Miss Mackle said, taking out the suntan lotion, the swimsuit, and the dark glasses. "Anything else?"

Song Lee and I raised our hands.

"Yes, Song Lee?"

"When Neil Armstrong and Buzz Aldrin walked on the moon, they played some golf."

"Great! So I can keep my golf clubs."

Everyone nodded.

"But you don't need that umbrella or

fan," Mary said. "It says in our green science book that it doesn't rain on the moon and there's no air to make a breeze." She sat back down.

Miss Mackle took out the umbrella and the fan.

"In fact," Mary added, "there's no water on the moon at all."

Harry jumped out of his seat. "*Wrong!*"

Mary stood up and pounded her desk. "I am *not!* It says so in our green science book. Page . . ." Everyone waited for Mary to find it. "Page 132!"

Everyone looked it up.

Even Sidney. "Yup! Says so right here. '*No water has been found on the moon.*' Mary's right. Harry's wrong. Case closed."

Miss Mackle waited.

"Song Lee and I got something different from the NASA Website," I said.

"What was that, Doug?" the teacher asked.

"It said NASA's Lunar Prospector collected evidence that could mean there's water on the moon."

Harry jumped out of his seat and held his hand high in the air. He looked like the Statue of Liberty. "I told you so!" Then he turned to Mary. "Your green science book FOOLED YA!"

Mary dropped the book on her desk.

"There's . . . water on the moon, Miss Mackle?" she asked.

"Most scientists think so. Exciting, huh? Our science books can't keep up with all the new discoveries!"

Song Lee and I read the printout from the computer together. "It's not liquid water, it's ice crystals. They believe the crystals are buried under the north and south poles on the moon."

"Man," Dexter said, running his fingers through his hair. "Ice on the moon. That's really cool!"

"But . . . how did the ice get there?" Mary asked.

"Comets," Harry replied. "Those dirty ice balls dive into the moon like . . ."

"*Neeeeyeow*," Sidney sang. He made his fist fly in the air, then take a nose-dive.

"You got it, Sid!" Harry replied. "And here's a picture of a comet," he added, showing Mary a cartoon he had cut out from the comics.

Mary looked, then plopped down in her chair. "So . . . what's a blue moon?

That wasn't in our green science book either."

Harry gladly explained. "It's when there are four full moons in a three month season. The third one is called a blue moon. It only happens every two and a half years. The science guy talked about it last week."

Miss Mackle clapped. "I'm so proud of you, class. You have collected so many fascinating facts about the moon, and you used different sources!"

Everyone cheered but Mary. She was pouting. Her bottom lip stuck out like a fat worm.

"So," Miss Mackle said. "Any suggestions for how we could celebrate?"

"I know how we could *if* I were rich," Harry groaned. Then he took out a piece of newspaper from his other jeans pocket. "It's an ad about a used telescope for sale."

"Really? How much?" Miss Mackle asked.

"Twenty-five dollars. It says it used to be in a small museum."

Song Lee started to jump up and down. "I've never looked through a telescope before!"

"Well," Harry said, "you can see the craters and seas with this baby!"

"Seas?" Sidney replied. "1 thought there was only buried ice on the moon."

Mary scowled. "Oh, Sid! If you did any reading at all, you would have known a sea is *not really* a sea on the moon. It's just a bunch of dark dust."

"No kidding!" Sidney replied. "Pretty tricky."

Miss Mackle looked at Harry's ad. "Do you think we could earn twenty-five dollars together and buy the telescope for our class?"

"Yes! Yes!" we all shouted.

Harry snapped his fingers. "That's my ticket to the moon!"

Mary dropped the fat worm off her mouth. "Maybe . . . we could each make something and have a bake sale, but call it a . . . moon sale!"

"What a great idea, Mary!" Miss Mackle exclaimed. "And after we earn enough money to buy the telescope, we can have a moonwatch at night, invite the parents, and see the moon!"

Everyone cheered and clapped.

Even Mary.

No one knew *then* what Harry was planning for the night of the moonwatch.

The Moon Sale

A few days before the moon sale, everybody talked about what they were going to make. Since it was Dexter and Sidney's turn, they were relaxing on the moon couch. Sid was taking a snooze.

"I'm baking big round sugar cookies," Mary announced. "Then I'm going to put yellow icing on them to make them look like full moons."

"I'm making Neil Armstrong cookies," I said.

"What are those?" Dexter asked.

"Peanut butter cookies, but instead of making a fork print on them before I put them in the oven, I'll step on them."

"That's gross," Mary replied.

"That's cool," Dexter said. "Just like Neil Armstrong's footprints on the moon."

"You've got it! So, what are you going to sell, Harry?" I asked.

"Something that doesn't cost anything, but is *the* most important thing on the moon."

"You can't bake something for nothing!" Mary said. "Sugar and flour and butter cost money."

"Who said I was baking?" Harry replied.

Mary put her nose in the air. "Who cares. We're making lots of money for the class telescope. No one is going to buy what *you* sell, Harry. It won't be worth anything."

"We'll see," Harry said.

The day of the moon sale finally came. Each one of us had made a poster of our favorite moon fact and hung it on a clothesline across the room.

Sidney's was a picture of a golf ball on the moon.

I got my desk ready and put up a little sign that said, *"Neil Armstrong Cookies 25¢."*

Dexter watched while I opened up my plastic container. "Mom wouldn't let me step on the cookies. She said we had to use our thumb and pinkie."

"Bummer," Dexter replied.

"I'm charging fifty cents each for my full moon cookies. They're big ones," Mary said. "Butter is expensive. Do you like the yellow sprinkles?"

"Bravissimo!" Mr. Cardini said as he strolled through the room. When he

looked around, he seemed puzzled. "Where's Harry?"

"He's coming," Mary said, making a face. "He has to get what he's selling out of the refrigerator downstairs."

"Hmmm," Mr. Cardini said, buying

one of everything. When he finished eating my peanut butter footprint, he licked his fingers. "Mmmmmm, *deeeeeeelicious*, but it sure makes me thirsty."

"Golf ball?" Sidney asked. "I've got two kinds. One has Neil Armstrong's autograph on it, the other has Buzz Aldrin's."

"That's forgery!" Mary sneered.

AUTO-
GRAPHED
GOLF BALLS

"I'll take two!" Mr. Cardini replied. "Where did you get that bucket of golf balls?"

"My stepdad used to live behind a golf course."

"Bravissimo!" Mr. Cardini exclaimed again.

Song Lee sold the principal an almond crescent cookie for twenty-five cents. It was shaped like the principal's mustache.

Harry finally showed up just as the second graders were coming into our room to buy goodies.

"Sorry for the delay, everybody! I'm here with the most important thing on the moon."

The second graders gathered around Harry's desk. We did too. We were curious about what Harry was selling that cost nothing to make.

"Ice." Harry grinned. "And I'll add some free water. Each cube is just a nickel. A real bargain."

"*Scusi!*" Mr. Cardini said, stepping in front of a second grader. "I'm so thirsty I can't stand it. Give me four cubes please."

Harry quickly counted on his fingers. Then he poured a thermos of water

into a large paper cup. "That's twenty cents, Mr. Cardini."

"Where did you get those cups?" Mary asked. "Paper cups cost money."

"Mrs. Funderburke in the cafeteria said she had extras. She didn't mind when I said it was for a good cause."

Mary rolled her eyes as she looked at the long line next to Harry's desk. Everyone wanted moon ice.

Then Mary looked at her twenty-three big yellow cookies. She had arranged them in four even rows of six, ten minutes ago. So far she had just sold one.

"Maybe fifty cents is too much. I'll sell them at a discount price," she said.

"Good idea," Ida replied.

Mary crossed out "50¢" and changed it to "49¢."

Fifteen minutes later, Harry was out of ice and water. "I sold every cube!" he bragged. "All sixty of them."

"Wow!" I said. "That's three dollars of *pure* profit!"

Mary slashed her original price in half. Now her sign said *"Full Moon Cookies 25¢."*

When it was all over, we counted up

the money we had earned and added it all together.

"Well, we have sixty-one dollars and fifty cents," Miss Mackle said. "We can buy that telescope *and* more moon books."

"The *newest* ones," Mary insisted.

"Yahoo!" Harry said. Then he added, "Hey you guys, I checked the newspaper. The full moon is next Wednesday night, October twenty-fourth. We should have our moonwatch then."

"Yes!" we all replied.

"Okay," Miss Mackle said. "I'll send home notices, and we'll hope for clear weather."

That's when Harry said it.

"I'm going to the moon that night, so I'm *praying* for good weather."

We all looked at Harry.

"Yeah, *right!*" Mary groaned.

The Moonwatch

October twenty-fourth finally came! It was time for our moonwatch.

It was dark.

It was clear.

It was cold.

It was exciting.

One by one we arrived on the playground at 6:30 P.M. My parents brought me. Mary brought a flashlight with a long handle. It looked like the kind that had four batteries. Ida and Song Lee came with Mr. and Mrs. Park. Dexter came with his teenage brother.

Sidney was wearing a funny jester winter cap. He was looking for the moon through his stepdad's binoculars, but it hadn't come up yet. There must have been fifty people if you counted the baby sisters and baby brothers. Even Mr. Cardini came.

One of the kids even had a little red telescope.

While we were lining up by the big old museum telescope, Miss Mackle was busy focusing it.

I looked around for Harry. He had said his grandmother was bringing him.

"Where's the moon?" Mary complained. "I can't see it."

"It'll be coming up soon behind that tree," Mr. Cardini said. "I saw it when I was driving over here. It looks like a huge pumpkin pie!"

"I think I see it!" Sidney said. "There in the tree!"

Mary shined her flashlight on it. "That's not the moon," Mary groaned. "It's a kickball."

While we were all standing in line to take a look through the telescope, Mr. Cardini started singing a song. He said it was called, "I'm Being Followed by a Moon Shadow."

It sounded kind of neat.

"Where's the moon!" Sidney snapped. He was running all over the playground like a madman. The tentacles on his jester cap had bells on the end and they were ringing like crazy!

Dexter took out his plastic guitar and began strumming it. "I love Elvis's song about the moon. It's called, 'When My Blue Moon Turns to Gold Again.'"

Miss Mackle kept trying to focus the big telescope. Mary was singing her own song: "I'm first in li-ne. I get to look fir-st."

It was annoying.

Sidney threw his hands in the air. "Moon! Where are you, moon! Come out! Come out or I'll . . . !"

Then suddenly it appeared over the oak tree.

"THE MOON!" we all screamed. It did look like a huge pumpkin pie high in the sky.

"THE MOON!" we screamed again.

Just then an old pickup truck with a bad muffler pulled up next to the school fence. I knew it was Harry! His grandmother got out with him.

"Look at the moon!" everyone shouted.

"Look at Harry!" I shouted back.

Everyone turned.

Harry was wearing a space suit. When he passed under the school porch light, we could see it was orange. Just like John Glenn's space suit.

He was even wearing a space helmet.

"Harry!" everyone called as we raced over to him.

"Why are you wearing that costume?" Mary asked.

"This isn't a costume. It's my space suit."

Mary took out her flashlight and shined it on Harry. "How come it says *Joe's Oil and Lube* on the back?"

Harry smiled. "Every space crew needs a good mechanic!"

Mary shined the flashlight on Harry's helmet. "That's the top of an old bubble-gum machine. You poked two breathing holes in it. One for your nose and one for your mouth."

"Out of my way," Harry said. "I'm about to make a lunar flight! I'm ready for takeoff!"

We watched Harry fly across the

playground. He had his hands in front of him like Superman. He circled the playground once and then ran over to the telescope. The line wasn't there anymore. Everyone was watching Harry. He took off his helmet and set it on the ground.

"10, 9, 8, 7, 6, 5, 4, 3, 2, 1, BLAST OFF! Oooooooh!" Harry said as he peered through the eyepiece of the telescope.

"Oooooh! Neat-o! I'm walking over
the craters. Yes! That dark spot is a
sea. I bet it's the Sea of Serenity where
Neil Armstrong landed. I'm walking in
the dark dust. I see the flag they left.
YES! YES! I'M ON THE MOON!"

Harry stepped aside and let Song
Lee take a turn. As soon as she looked
through the telescope, she oohed and

aaahed. *"I'm on the moon!"* she exclaimed. "It's so beautiful. It's so sandy looking. I'm walking on it now just like Harry did!"

When I took a turn, I found myself saying the same thing. It seemed so real. "Wow! I can touch that crater. I can see that sea! I'm walking on the dark dust. Are those Neil Armstrong's footprints?"

"Hurry up!" Sidney said. "I want to see if I can find the golf ball."

Harry put his helmet back on and soared across the playground. Every time he stopped and looked up at the moon, he leaped high in the air. "TO THE MOON!" he shouted. Song Lee and I followed him around, leaping and jumping.

Mary shook her head. "Harry

Spooger is a *big* wacko. Finally, it's my turn to look through the telescope. I think Harry did that whole space act just to butt in front of me. I *was* first in line. Harry got to look through the telescope first. Old remainder himself!"

When Mary looked through the telescope, she finally stopped talking.

Everyone else was running around the playground. "Look!" Harry said. "There's mountains on the moon!"

"I can't see anything," Mary com-

plained as she kept looking through the eyepiece of the telescope. "It's out of focus."

Miss Mackle came over and tried to help. "I had it focused just a minute ago. This old telescope is very temperamental."

Mr. Cardini chuckled. "I don't think it matters anymore. Harry will take you to the moon."

"*Puleeeeze,*" Mary groaned. She wasn't buying it.

But I did. And so did the rest of the kids.

Harry made us *feel* like we were on the moon that night. And that's almost like being there.